I AM READING

Doc Witch's Animal Hospital

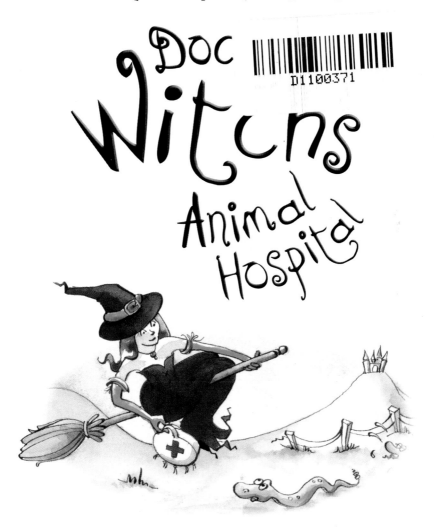

SHEILA MAY BIRD

Illustrated by
EMMA PARRISH

MACMILLAN CHILDREN'S BOOKS

To Mum, who still likes to hear my stories S.M.B.
For my mum, with oodles of love E.P.

First published 2007 by Kingfisher

This edition published 2011 by Macmillan Children's Books
a division of Macmillan Publishers Limited
20 New Wharf Road, London N1 9RR
Basingstoke and Oxford
Associated companies throughout the world
www.panmacmillan.com

ISBN 978-1-4472-0928-7

Text copyright © Sheila May Bird 2007
Illustrations copyright © Emma Parrish 2007

The right of Sheila May Bird and Emma Parrish to be identified
as the author and illustrator of this work has been asserted by them
in accordance with the Copyright, Designs and Patents Act 1988

3 5 7 9 8 6 4 2

A CIP catalogue record for this book is available from the British Library.

Printed in China

Contents

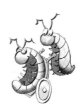

Chapter One

Doctor Imelda Witch lived in a pretty cottage. It had a curved roof and a crooked chimney.

Around the cottage was a garden where Doctor Witch grew the plants for her spells and potions, ointments and lotions. It was a pretty garden, but a rather smelly one too.

Doctor Witch's Animal Hospital

Doctor Witch arrived back at her cottage after a very busy morning. She had been helping a woodlouse give birth to 130 baby woodlice.

Doctor Witch was a vet – a special doctor who looks after animals.

Now her cottage was full of animals, all waiting to see her.

"First please," she called.

"That's me," said a very tiny voice.

Clomp, clomp, ouch, clomp, clomp . . .

"Ah, Mr Centipede," said Doctor Witch, looking down. "How can I help you?"

"I've hurt my leg," replied the centipede. He painfully waved one of his many legs at her.

With a twitch of her nose and a flick of
her wand . . .

. . . Doctor Witch shrank herself to the
size of the centipede.

"Oh dear," said Doctor Witch. "I'm afraid your leg is broken. But with my spells and potions, ointments and lotions, I'm sure I can help."

She mixed a potion and plastered the broken leg.

"It's just as well you've got 99 other legs to use," she said.

The grateful centipede left.

Clomp, clomp, clomp, clomp, thud, clomp, clomp . . .

"Next please," called Doctor Witch.

Chapter Two

That day Doctor Witch used her spells
and potions, ointments and lotions to
help:

A badger with
bad breath . . .

. . . a deer with
dizziness . . .

. . . a fox with flu . . .

. . . a weasel with a
wobbly tooth . . .

. . . a rabbit with
a rash . . .

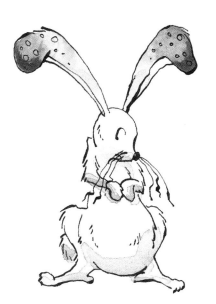

. . . and a squirrel
with a squint.

She shut the door as her last patient left.

An owl flew into it.

"Ouch!" said the owl. "I think I've broken my beak."

"I'm very sorry," said Doctor Witch. She looked at the owl's beak. It looked sore, but it was not broken.

The owl gave Doctor
Witch her invitation.
"For me?" said Doctor
Witch. "How exciting!"

You are invited to the annual
Wizard and Witch ball.
It is this Saturday at
The Grand Hall.
Please reply using
the delivery owl.

Doctor Witch
was delighted.

She wrote a reply. "Yes
please! I would love to
come. Thank you!"

Chapter Three

Doctor Witch was very excited.

The important question was, what would

she wear?

She could wear the long, straight,

jet-black dress.

She might wear
the long, flowing,
night-black dress.

She definitely
wouldn't wear the
short, frilly, coal-black
dress, because it showed
her knobbly knees!

Which hat should she wear? Bendy points were popular, but she had always favoured a tall, slender point.

She went to bed dreaming of handsome
wizards and chocolate cake.

The next morning Doctor Witch mixed together some wild flowers in her cauldron.

She mixed Toad's Foot and Hare's Bell . . .

. . . with some Old Man's Beard . . .

. . . and added some Bird's
Foot for good measure.

Then she put the potion into
a bottle ready for her bath
on Saturday.

Saturday came quickly. Doctor Witch
enjoyed getting ready for the ball.
She took the frogs and newts out of the
bath before she used it.
She poured the potion into the hot water,
making rainbow-coloured bubbles.

She polished her black nails . . .

. . . her black boots . . .

. . . and even her black tooth.

Once she was dressed, she looked into her
magic mirror.

"Mirror, mirror, on the wall,
how do I look?"

"Not bad at all!" it replied.

She gave herself a satisfied smile and
fetched her broomstick from the shed.
Then she packed a selection of spells and
potions, ointments and lotions into her
portable first-aid kit.

In no time at all, she was off to the ball.

Chapter Four

She hadn't flown far when she heard a
worried hiss from the grass below.
"Pleasssse come to ssssee my baby.
He hassss bitten hissss own tongue."
With a twitch of her nose and a flick of
her wand Doctor Witch was the size of a
snake. She followed the mother snake
through the grass.

"Don't worry. With my spells and potions, ointments and lotions, I'll soon have your tongue fixed," she told the baby snake.

And she did.

"You're *sssso* kind," hissed the snakes.

With a twitch of her nose and a flick of
her wand Doctor Witch was back on her
way to the ball. But now her tall, slender-
pointed hat was bent. She had grass seeds
in her hair and mud on her face.

"Bother!" she said, when she caught sight
of herself in a puddle.

She hadn't gone far when she heard
another noise. In a tall tree two owls
were flapping in their nest.
"Up here!" they hooted. "Up here!"
Doctor Witch pointed her
broomstick towards the tree.

"Our baby has fallen out of the nest!" cried the owls.

Doctor Imelda Witch could see the baby owl caught in the lower branches of a tree.

"I can't do a lot with spells
and potions, ointments and
lotions. But I think I can
reach him with my
broomstick," she said.

By weaving the broomstick through the
branches Doctor Witch was able to rescue
the fallen bird. She took him back to his
nest.

"Thank you, thank you," hooted the grateful owls.

"You're welcome," she replied.

But now her dress was torn and she had lost one of her well-polished black boots. "Bother! Bother!" she said.

Chapter Five

Doctor Witch arrived at the ball. She was rather late. Her dress was torn and her pointed hat was bent. One of her shoes was missing. She had grass seeds in her hair. She had mud on her face.

But worst of all, she had lost her wand!

"Oh very big bothers!" she said.

She showed her crumpled invitation to the wizard at the door.

"You can't come in here looking like that," he said. "Go away."

She had been looking forward to meeting handsome wizards. She had been looking forward to eating chocolate cake even more.

Poor Doctor Witch. She had only been trying to be helpful.

Without her wand she couldn't even cast a clean-up spell.

Chapter Six

One of the owls, whose baby Doctor
Witch had rescued, landed on the wizard's
shoulder. It cooed hurriedly into his ear.

"I say," called the wizard to Doctor
Witch, "this owl says that you saved
his baby."

"All part of a day's work,"
replied Doctor Witch
modestly.

42

There was a rustling around the wizard's
feet and much muffled hissing.

"Mrs Snake says that you stopped her
baby's tongue bleeding," said the wizard.
"It was the least I could do," said Doctor
Witch sincerely.
"Any witch as caring as you have been
deserves to go to the ball," said the
wizard.

"Excuse me," said a very small voice from the wizard's toe, "I found this. I think it belongs to the vet." The centipede with the plastered leg had a wand balanced on his back.

"Oh thank you!" cried Doctor Witch.
And with a twitch of her nose and a flick
of her wand, she looked clean and tidy
again.

Doctor Witch had a wonderful time. She
danced with handsome wizards until her
feet ached and she had to take off her
well-polished boots.

But best of all, Doctor Witch ate a lot of
chocolate cake.

About the Author and Illustrator

Sheila May Bird used to work as a nanny and a nursery nurse. Nowadays she enjoys writing children's stories, "I wish I could twitch my nose and do magic like Doctor Witch," she says. Sheila lives in Warlingham, Surrey.

Emma Parrish has had several children's books published. Emma says, "I was so pleased Doctor Witch enjoyed the ball in the end. She deserved it after being so kind to the animals." Emma was born and still lives in Wales, in a beautiful old farmhouse with her sheepdog, Leah.

Tips for Beginner Readers

1. Think about the cover and the title of the book. What do you think it will be about? While you are reading, think about what might happen next and why.

2. As you read, ask yourself if what you're reading makes sense. If it doesn't, try rereading or look at the pictures for clues.

3. If there is a word that you do not know, look carefully at the letters, sounds, and word parts that you do know. Blend the sounds to read the word. Is this a word you know? Does it make sense in the sentence?

4. Think about the characters, where the story takes place, and the problems the characters in the story faced. What are the important ideas in the beginning, middle and end of the story?

5. Ask yourself questions like:
Did you like the story?
Why or why not?
How did the author make it fun to read?
How well did you understand it?

Maybe you can understand the story better if you read it again!